EVERY LIVING THING

EVERY LIVING THING

STORIES BY
Cynthia Rylant

DECORATIONS BY
S.D. Schindler

Aladdin Paperbacks

Aladdin Paperbacks
An imprint of Simon & Schuster
Children's Publishing Division
1230 Avenue of the Americas
New York, NY 10020
Copyright © 1985 by Cynthia Rylant
All rights reserved including the right of reproduction in whole or in part in any form.
First Aladdin Paperbacks edition, 1988
Also available in a hardcover edition from
Simon & Schuster Books for Young Readers
Printed and bound in the United States of America

20

Rylant, Cynthia.
Every living thing/stories by Cynthia Rylant; decorations by
S.D. Schindler.—1st Aladdin books ed.
p.   cm.
Summary: Twelve stories in which animals change people's lives for the better.
ISBN 0-689-71263-4
1. Children's stories, American.   [1. Animals—Fiction.
2. Animals—Fiction.   3. Pets—Therapeutic use—Fiction.   4. Short stories.]   I. Schindler, S.D., ill.   II. Title.
[PZ7.R982Er 1988]
[Fic]—dc19   88-19359   CIP   AC

For Gerry
and all the living things we have loved

Contents

And of every living thing of
all flesh, two of every sort shalt
thou bring into the ark, to
keep them alive with thee . . .

GENESIS 6:19
The Holy Bible

Slower Than the Rest

Leo was the first one to spot the turtle, so he was the one who got to keep it. They had all been in the car, driving up Tyler Mountain to church, when Leo shouted, "There's a turtle!" and everyone's head jerked with the stop.

Leo's father grumbled something about turtle soup, but Leo's mother was sympathetic toward turtles, so Leo was allowed to pick it up off the highway and bring it home. Both his little sisters squealed when the animal stuck its ugly head out to look at them, and they thought its claws horrifying, but Leo loved it from the start. He named it Charlie.

The dogs at Leo's house had always belonged more to Leo's father than to anyone else, and the cat thought she belonged to no one but herself, so Leo was grateful for a pet of his own. He settled Charlie in a cardboard box, threw in some lettuce and radishes, and declared himself a happy boy.

Leo adored Charlie, and the turtle was hugged and kissed as if he were a baby. Leo liked to fit Charlie's shell on his shoulder under his left ear, just as one might carry a cat, and Charlie would poke his head into Leo's neck now and then to keep them both entertained.

Leo was ten years old the year he found Charlie. He hadn't many friends because he was slower than the rest. That was the way his father said it: "Slower than the rest." Leo was slow in reading, slow in numbers, slow in understanding nearly everything that passed before him in a classroom. As a result, in fourth grade Leo had been separated from the rest of his classmates and placed in a room with other children who were as slow as he. Leo thought he would never get over it. He saw no way to be happy after that.

But Charlie took care of Leo's happiness, and he did it by being congenial. Charlie was the friendliest turtle anyone had ever seen. The turtle's head was always stretched out, moving left to right, trying to see what was in the world. His front and back legs moved as though he were swimming frantically in a deep sea to save himself, when all that was happening was that someone was holding him in midair. Put Charlie down and he would sniff at the air a moment, then take off as if no one had ever told him how slow he was supposed to be.

Every day, Leo came home from school, took Charlie to the backyard to let him explore and told him about the things that had happened in fifth grade. Leo wasn't sure how old Charlie was, and, though he guessed Charlie was probably a young turtle, the lines around Charlie's forehead and eyes and the clamp of his mouth made Leo think Charlie was wise the way old people are wise. So Leo talked to him privately every day.

Then one day Leo decided to take Charlie to school.

It was Prevent Forest Fires week and the whole school was making posters, watching nature films, imitating Smokey the Bear. Each member of Leo's class was assigned to give a report on Friday dealing with forests. So Leo brought Charlie.

Leo was quiet about it on the bus to school. He held the covered box tightly on his lap, secretly relieved that turtles are quiet except for an occasional hiss. Charlie rarely hissed in the morning; he was a turtle who liked to sleep in.

Leo carried the box to his classroom and placed it on the wide windowsill near the radiator and beside the geraniums. His teacher called attendance and the day began.

In the middle of the morning, the forest reports began. One girl held up a poster board pasted with pictures of raccoons and squirrels, rabbits and deer, and she explained that animals died in forest fires. The pictures were too small for anyone to see from his desk. Leo was bored.

One boy stood up and mumbled something about burnt-up trees. Then another got up and said if there were no forests, then his dad couldn't go hunting, and Leo couldn't see the connection in that at all.

Finally it was his turn. He quietly walked over to the windowsill and picked up the box. He set it on the teacher's desk.

"When somebody throws a match into a forest," Leo began, "he is a murderer. He kills trees and birds and animals. Some animals, like deer, are fast runners and they might escape. But other animals"— he lifted the cover off the box—"have no hope. They are too slow. They will die." He lifted Charlie out of the box. "It isn't fair," he said, as the class gasped and giggled at what they saw. "It isn't fair for the slow ones."

Leo said much more. Mostly he talked about Charlie, explained what turtles were like, the things they enjoyed, what talents they possessed. He talked about Charlie the turtle and Charlie the friend, and what he said and how he said it made everyone in the class love turtles and hate forest fires. Leo's teacher had tears in her eyes.

That afternoon, the whole school assembled in the gymnasium to bring the special week to a close. A ranger in uniform made a speech, then someone dressed up like Smokey the Bear danced with two others dressed up like squirrels. Leo sat with his box and wondered if he should laugh at the dancers with everyone else. He didn't feel like it.

Finally, the school principal stood up and began a long talk. Leo's thoughts drifted off. He thought about being home, lying in his bed and drawing pictures, while Charlie hobbled all about the room.

He did not hear when someone whispered his name. Then he jumped when he heard, "Leo! It's you!" in his ear. The boy next to him was pushing him, making him get up.

"What?" Leo asked, looking around in confusion.

"You won!" they were all saying. "Go on!"

Leo was pushed onto the floor. He saw the principal smiling at him, beckoning to him across the room. Leo's legs moved like Charlie's—quickly and forward.

Leo carried the box tightly against his chest. He shook the principal's hand. He put down the box to accept the award plaque being handed to him. It was for his presentation with Charlie. Leo had won an award for the first time in his life, and as he shook the principal's hand and blushed and said his thank-you's, he thought his heart would explode with happiness.

That night, alone in his room, holding Charlie on his shoulder, Leo felt proud. And for the first time in a long time, Leo felt *fast*.

Retired

Her name was Miss Phala Cutcheon and she used to be a schoolteacher. Miss Cutcheon had gotten old and had retired from teaching fourth grade, so now she simply sat on her porch and considered things. She considered moving to Florida. She considered joining a club for old people and learning to play cards. She considered dying.

Finally, she just got a dog.

The dog was old. And she, too, was retired. A retired collie. She had belonged to a family who lived around the corner from Miss Cutcheon. The dog had helped raise three children, and she had been loved. But the family was moving to France and could not take their beloved pet. They gave her to Miss Cutcheon.

When she lived with the family, the dog's name had been Princess. Miss Cutcheon, however, thought the name much too delicate for a dog as old and bony as Miss Cutcheon herself, and she changed it to Velma. It took Princess several days to figure out what Miss Cutcheon meant when she called out for someone named Velma.

In time, though, Velma got used to her new name. She got used to Miss Cutcheon's slow pace—so unlike the romping of three children—and she got used to Miss Cutcheon's dry dog food. She learned not to mind the smell of burning asthmador, which helped Miss Cutcheon breathe better, and not to mind the sound of the old lady's wheezing and snoring in the middle of the night. Velma missed her children, but she was all right.

Miss Cutcheon was a very early riser (a habit that could not be broken after forty-three years of meeting children at the schoolhouse door), and she enjoyed big breakfasts. Each day Miss

Cutcheon would creak out of her bed like a mummy rising from its tomb, then shuffle into the kitchen, straight for the coffee pot. Velma, who slept on the floor at the end of Miss Cutcheon's bed, would soon creak off the floor herself and head into the kitchen. Velma's family had eaten cold cereal breakfasts all those years, and only when she came to live with Miss Cutcheon did Velma realize what perking coffee, sizzling bacon and hot biscuits smell like. She still got only dry dog food, but the aromas around her nose made the chunks taste ten times better.

Miss Cutcheon sat at her dinette table, eating her bacon and eggs and biscuits, sipping her coffee, while Velma lay under the table at her feet. Miss Cutcheon spent most of breakfast time thinking about all the children she had taught. Velma thought about hers.

During the day Miss Cutcheon took Velma for walks up and down the block. The two of them became a familiar sight. On warm, sunny days they took many walks, moving at an almost brisk pace up and back. But on damp, cold days they eased themselves along the sidewalk as if they'd both just gotten out of bed, and they usually went only a half-block, morning and afternoon.

Miss Cutcheon and Velma spent several months together like this: eating breakfast together, walking the block, sitting on the front porch, going to bed early. Velma's memory of her three children grew fuzzy, and only when she saw a boy or girl passing on the street did her ears prick up as if she *should* have known something about children. But what it was she had forgotten.

Miss Cutcheon's memory, on the other hand, grew better every day, and she seemed not to know anything except the past. She could recite the names of children in her mind—which seats they had sat in, what subjects they were best at, what they'd brought to school for lunch. She could remember their funny ways, and sometimes she would be sitting at her dinette in the morning, quietly eating, when she would burst out with a laugh that filled the room and made Velma jump.

Why Miss Cutcheon decided one day to walk Velma a few blocks farther, and to the west, is a puzzle. But one warm morning in September, they did walk that way, and when they reached the third block, a sound like a million tiny buzz saws floated into the air. Velma's ears stood straight up, and Miss Cutcheon stopped and considered. Then they went a block farther, and the sound changed to something like a hundred bells pealing. Velma's tail began to wag ever so slightly. Finally, in the fifth block, they saw the school playground.

Children, small and large, ran wildly about, screaming, laughing, falling down, climbing up, jumping, dancing. Velma started barking, again and again and again. She couldn't contain herself. She barked and wagged and forgot all about Miss Cutcheon standing there with her. She saw only the children and it made her happy.

Miss Cutcheon stood very stiff a while, staring. She didn't smile. She simply looked at the playground, the red brick school, the chain-link fence that protected it all, keeping intruders outside, keeping children inside. Miss Cutcheon just stared while Velma barked. Then they walked back home.

But the next day they returned. They moved farther along the fence, nearer where the children were. Velma barked and wagged until two boys, who had been seesawing, ran over to the fence to try to pet the dog. Miss Cutcheon pulled back on the leash, but too late, for Velma had already leaped up against the wire. She poked her snout through a hole and the boys scratched it, laughing as she licked their fingers. More children came to the fence, and while some rubbed Velma's nose, others questioned Miss Cutcheon: "What's your dog's name?" "Will it bite?" "Do you like cats?" Miss Cutcheon, who had not answered the questions of children in what seemed a very long time, replied as a teacher would.

Every day, in good weather, Miss Cutcheon and Velma visited the playground fence. The children learned their names, and Miss Cutcheon soon knew the children who stroked Velma the way she had known her own fourth-graders years ago. In bad weather, Miss Cutcheon and Velma stayed inside, breathing the asthmadora, feeling warm and comfortable, thinking about the children at the playground. But on a nice day, they were out again.

In mid-October, Miss Cutcheon put a pumpkin on her front porch, something she hadn't done in years. And on Halloween night, she turned on the porch light, and she and Velma waited at the door. Miss Cutcheon passed out fifty-six chocolate bars before the evening was done.

Then, on Christmas Eve of that same year, a large group of young carolers came to sing in front of Miss Cutcheon's house; and they were bearing gifts of dog biscuits and sweet fruit.

Boar Out There

Everyone in Glen Morgan knew there was a wild boar in the woods over by the Miller farm. The boar was out beyond the splintery rail fence and past the old black Dodge that somehow had ended up in the woods and was missing most of its parts.

Jenny would hook her chin over the top rail of the fence, twirl a long green blade of grass in her teeth and whisper, "Boar out there."

And there were times she was sure she heard

him. She imagined him running heavily through the trees, ignoring the sharp thorns and briars that raked his back and sprang away trembling.

She thought he might have a golden horn on his terrible head. The boar would run deep into the woods, then rise up on his rear hooves, throw his head toward the stars and cry a long, clear, sure note into the air. The note would glide through the night and spear the heart of the moon. The boar had no fear of the moon, Jenny knew, as she lay in bed, listening.

One hot summer day she went to find the boar. No one in Glen Morgan had ever gone past the old black Dodge and beyond, as far as she knew. But the boar was there somewhere, between those awful trees, and his dark green eyes waited for someone.

Jenny felt it was she.

Moving slowly over damp brown leaves, Jenny could sense her ears tingle and fan out as she listened for thick breathing from the trees. She stopped to pick a teaberry leaf to chew, stood a minute, then went on.

Deep in the woods she kept her eyes to the sky. She needed to be reminded that there was a world above and apart from the trees—a world of space and air, air that didn't linger all about her, didn't press deep into her skin, as forest air did.

Finally, leaning against a tree to rest, she heard him for the first time. She forgot to breathe, standing there listening to the stamping of hooves, and she choked and coughed.

Coughed!

And now the pounding was horrible, too loud and confusing for Jenny. Horrible. She stood stiff with wet eyes and knew she could always pray, but for some reason didn't.

He came through the trees so fast that she had no time to scream or run. And he was there before her.

His large gray-black body shivered as he waited just beyond the shadow of the tree she held for support. His nostrils glistened, and his eyes; but astonishingly, he was silent. He shivered and glistened and was absolutely silent.

Jenny matched his silence, and her body was rigid, but not her eyes. They traveled along his scarred, bristling back to his thick hind legs. Tears spilling and flooding her face, Jenny stared at the boar's ragged ears, caked with blood. Her tears dropped to the leaves, and the only sound between them was his slow breathing.

17

Then the boar snorted and jerked. But Jenny did not move.

High in the trees a bluejay yelled, and, suddenly, it was over. Jenny stood like a rock as the boar wildly flung his head and in terror bolted past her.

Past her. . . .

And now, since that summer, Jenny still hooks her chin over the old rail fence, and she still whispers, "Boar out there." But when she leans on the fence, looking into the trees, her eyes are full and she leaves wet patches on the splintery wood. She is sorry for the torn ears of the boar and sorry that he has no golden horn.

But mostly she is sorry that he lives in fear of bluejays and little girls, when everyone in Glen Morgan lives in fear of him.

Papa's Parrot

Though his father was fat and merely owned a candy and nut shop, Harry Tillian liked his papa. Harry stopped liking candy and nuts when he was around seven, but, in spite of this, he and Mr. Tillian had remained friends and were still friends the year Harry turned twelve.

For years, after school, Harry had always stopped in to see his father at work. Many of Harry's friends stopped there, too, to spend a few cents choosing penny candy from the giant

19

bins or to sample Mr. Tillian's latest batch of roasted peanuts. Mr. Tillian looked forward to seeing his son and his son's friends every day. He liked the company.

When Harry entered junior high school, though, he didn't come by the candy and nut shop as often. Nor did his friends. They were older and they had more spending money. They went to a burger place. They played video games. They shopped for records. None of them were much interested in candy and nuts anymore.

A new group of children came to Mr. Tillian's shop now. But not Harry Tillian and his friends.

The year Harry turned twelve was also the year Mr. Tillian got a parrot. He went to a pet store one day and bought one for more money than he could really afford. He brought the parrot to his shop, set its cage near the sign for maple clusters and named it Rocky.

Harry thought this was the strangest thing his father had ever done, and he told him so, but Mr. Tillian just ignored him.

Rocky was good company for Mr. Tillian. When business was slow, Mr. Tillian would turn on a small color television he had sitting in a corner, and he and Rocky would watch the soap operas. Rocky liked to scream when the romantic music came on, and Mr. Tillian would yell at him to shut up, but they seemed to enjoy themselves.

The more Mr. Tillian grew to like his parrot, and the more he talked to it instead of to people, the more embarrassed Harry became. Harry would stroll past the shop, on his way somewhere else, and he'd take a quick look inside to see what his dad was doing. Mr. Tillian was always talking to the bird. So Harry kept walking.

At home things were different. Harry and his father joked with each other at the dinner table as they always had—Mr. Tillian teasing Harry about his smelly socks; Harry teasing Mr. Tillian about his blubbery stomach. At home things seemed all right.

But one day, Mr. Tillian became ill. He had been at work, unpacking boxes of caramels, when he had grabbed his chest and fallen over on top of the candy. A customer had found him, and he was taken to the hospital in an ambulance.

Mr. Tillian couldn't leave the hospital. He lay in bed, tubes in his arms, and he worried about his shop. New shipments of candy and nuts would be arriving. Rocky would be hungry. Who would take care of things?

Harry said he would. Harry told his father that he would go to the store every day after school and unpack boxes. He would sort out all the candy and nuts. He would even feed Rocky.

So, the next morning, while Mr. Tillian lay in his hospital bed, Harry took the shop key to school with him. After school he left his friends and walked to the empty shop alone. In all the days of his life, Harry had never seen the shop closed after school. Harry didn't even remember what the CLOSED sign looked like. The key stuck in the lock three times, and inside he had to search all the walls for the light switch.

The shop was as his father had left it. Even the caramels were still spilled on the floor. Harry bent down and picked them up one by one, dropping them back in the boxes. The bird in its cage watched him silently.

Harry opened the new boxes his father

22

hadn't gotten to. Peppermints. Jawbreakers. Toffee creams. Strawberry kisses. Harry traveled from bin to bin, putting the candies where they belonged.

"Hello!"

Harry jumped, spilling a box of jawbreakers.

"Hello, Rocky!"

Harry stared at the parrot. He had forgotten it was there. The bird had been so quiet, and Harry had been thinking only of the candy.

"Hello," Harry said.

"Hello, Rocky!" answered the parrot.

Harry walked slowly over to the cage. The parrot's food cup was empty. Its water was dirty. The bottom of the cage was a mess.

Harry carried the cage into the back room.

"Hello, Rocky!"

"Is that all you can say, you dumb bird?" Harry mumbled. The bird said nothing else.

Harry cleaned the bottom of the cage, refilled the food and water cups, then put the cage back in its place and resumed sorting the candy.

"Where's Harry?"

Harry looked up.

"Where's Harry?"

Harry stared at the parrot.

"Where's Harry?"

Chills ran down Harry's back. What could the bird mean? It was like something from "The Twilight Zone."

"Where's Harry?"

Harry swallowed and said, "I'm here. I'm here, you stupid bird."

"You stupid bird!" said the parrot.

Well, at least he's got one thing straight, thought Harry.

"Miss him! Miss him! Where's Harry? You stupid bird!"

Harry stood with a handful of peppermints.

"*What?*" he asked.

"Where's Harry?" said the parrot.

"I'm *here*, you stupid bird! I'm here!" Harry yelled. He threw the peppermints at the cage, and the bird screamed and clung to its perch.

Harry sobbed, "I'm here." The tears were coming.

Harry leaned over the glass counter.

"Papa." Harry buried his face in his arms.

"Where's Harry?" repeated the bird.

Harry sighed and wiped his face on his sleeve. He watched the parrot. He understood now:

someone had been saying, for a long time, "Where's Harry? Miss him."

Harry finished his unpacking, then swept the floor of the shop. He checked the furnace so the bird wouldn't get cold. Then he left to go visit his papa.

A Pet

The year she was ten, Emmanuella—Emma for short—begged so hard for a Christmas pet that her parents finally relented and gave her the next best thing: a goldfish. Her father, who was a lawyer, had argued for years that money could buy better things than flea collars, that Emma did not need a pet, that Emma had seen too many Walt Disney movies. Her mother, also a lawyer, argued that Emma should spend time with her viola, not with an animal. But that December, her parents decided to end the debate. They bought a goldfish and an aquarium from a young man who was moving out of town. They got the goldfish cheap because used goldfish are hard to unload onto someone else, but mainly because this particular goldfish was old and blind.

Even Emma's parents couldn't stoop to giving her a used aquarium with a used fish in it on Christmas morning, so, instead, on the tenth day of December they put the tank in her room, where she found it after school.

When Emma dropped her books on her bed, she took one look toward the corner and said, "What on earth?" At first she couldn't even imagine why an aquarium would be in her room. The word "fish" was so far away from the word "pet." But her parents explained cheerfully that indeed the fish was the pet she had asked for, and Emma understood ruefully that it would be a fish or nothing.

The fish came already named by its former owner, who had called it Joshua. Emma didn't mind the name. In fact, for a wrinkled, sightless, overgrown goldfish, most names just wouldn't have seemed right. Joshua, at least, was a natural name—old and natural.

In time, Emma came to like the fish after all.

At night, with the water glowing blue and Joshua moving serenely—reflections of yellow and gold and orange—above the pink gravel, it seemed to Emma she had never seen anything so pretty. She watched her aquarium the way astronomers watch stars.

And Emma couldn't help becoming fond of Joshua. The white, creamy film covering his eyes made him look always confused and at loose ends. He sometimes made bold dashes around the tank as if he had some purpose in life, a job to do. On other days, he lolled about lazily, barely moving his fins, depending more on the water than on himself to keep his body afloat. Those lazy days, he had a habit of bumping his head into a plastic plant or colliding with his castle.

Emma watched him and felt she knew him. When she raised the squeaky lid of the aquarium to shake some shrimp flakes onto the water, Joshua jumped up and came to the top, just as cats and dogs will come running when their food dishes are being filled. Joshua had to guess where the flakes were as they lay on the surface, and he took several gulps of water when he missed. Emma laughed at him.

Joshua had lived with Emma nearly five

months when one day in April she noticed Joshua's tail fin looked shabby, like a hair comb that was missing some teeth.

The next day his tail fin looked worse, and he wobbled when he swam, as if he needed a cane.

Emma was growing worried.

Then, the third day, there were white spots on Joshua's scales. He leaned his body against the side of the tank and rested. He did not dash and he did not loll. He leaned and rested.

Emma rushed to the pet store after school and brought home a box of medicine. In the aquarium Joshua lay on his side. Sometimes he tried to move to a different part of the tank, but he couldn't swim and he just fell over again.

Emma dropped two pills into the water.

"Please," she whispered. "Please."

Late into the night, Emma watched as Joshua lay ill. Sometimes she cried. Once she sprinkled some shrimp flakes into the tank, but they just floated down to the bottom, settling on the gravel around Joshua.

In the morning, Joshua was dead. Emma found him floating on top of the water when she woke up. When she lifted him out of the water in the net, it surprised her how heavy he was. He was as large as her hand, and it surprised her because she had never held him.

For a few moments, she petted him, as she had not ever been able to do. Then she buried him in the backyard, along with his castle. Her parents watched her from a window, inside the house.

Spaghetti

It was evening, and people sat outside, talking quietly among themselves. On the stoop of a tall building of crumbling bricks and rotting wood sat a boy. His name was Gabriel and he wished for some company.

Gabriel was thinking about things. He remembered being the only boy in class with the right answer that day, and he remembered the butter sandwich he had had for lunch. Gabriel was thinking that he would like to live outside all the time. He imagined himself carrying a

pack of food and a few tools and a heavy cloth
to erect a hasty tent. Gabriel saw himself sleeping among coyotes. But next he saw himself
sleeping beneath the glittering lights of a movie
theater, near the bus stop.

Gabriel was a boy who thought about things
so seriously, so fully, that on this evening he
nearly missed hearing a cry from the street.
The cry was so weak and faraway in his mind
that, for him, it could have been the slow lift-
ing of a stubborn window. It could have been
the creak of an old man's legs. It could have
been the wind.

But it was not the wind, and it came to Gabriel slowly that he did, indeed, hear something, and that it did, indeed, sound like a cry
from the street.

Gabriel picked himself up from the stoop
and began to walk carefully along the edge of
the street, peering into the gloom and the dusk.
The cry came again and Gabriel's ears tingled
and he walked faster.

He stared into the street, up and down it,
knowing something was there. The street was
so gray that he could not see. . . . But not only
the street was gray.

There, sitting on skinny stick-legs, wobbling

to and fro, was a tiny gray kitten. No cars had passed to frighten it, and so it just sat in the street and cried its windy, creaky cry and waited.

Gabriel was amazed. He had never imagined he would be lucky enough one day to find a kitten. He walked into the street and lifted the kitten into his hands.

Gabriel sat on the sidewalk with the kitten next to his cheek and thought. The kitten smelled of pasta noodles, and he wondered if it belonged to a friendly Italian man somewhere in the city. Gabriel called the kitten Spaghetti.

Gabriel and Spaghetti returned to the stoop. It occurred to Gabriel to walk the neighborhood and look for the Italian man, but the purring was so loud, so near his ear, that he could not think as seriously, as fully, as before.

Gabriel no longer wanted to live outside. He knew he had a room and a bed of his own in the tall building. So he stood up, with Spaghetti under his chin, and went inside to show his kitten where they would live together.

Drying Out

Jack Mitchell had fought in a war, run a gas station, preached the gospel on the side and raised two boys. Then his wife left him because she said she wanted to find herself. She went to live on a college campus and told him not to bother her anymore.

Jack no longer had a war, a gas station, the gospel, the boys or now even a wife.

He started drinking, spending all his money on whiskey. He'd load up in a bar, then pass out somewhere on the way home. In the morning he'd find himself huddled behind some bushes next to the library or stretched out on the porch of a church. In stinking clothes, he'd drag home, full of shame.

Jack would then clean himself up, go to church the next Sunday and swear he'd never take another drink.

But in a week or two, he'd do it all again.

One night Jack was arrested. A policeman found him lying in a sandbox in the park. Jack had to pay a fine and was ordered by the judge to go to the Veterans Hospital to "dry out."

Jack checked himself in the next week.

The Veterans Hospital was on the edge of town, surrounded by green lawns and bordering a forest. The yellow brick building was old, and inside, on its walls, were framed mementos of all the wars that had made its patients veterans: pictures of generals and troops, plaques remembering some who had died, framed newspaper articles describing victory in battle, American flags. It was a hospital filled mostly with men; and these men had been lucky enough to survive their wars, but not lucky enough to leave them behind. Many of the patients had missing arms or legs; many suffered with diseases they had caught as young soldiers in foreign countries. And many, like Jack, suffered because they could not stop drinking.

Jack knew when he checked in that he would not be leaving the hospital for weeks. He would stay until the doctors were satisfied he wouldn't drink anymore. More than anything, it was giving up his freedom that he hated. Giving up the whiskey would be hard—but feeling trapped inside that hospital meant pure misery.

When the squirrels came, Jack had been in the hospital about a week and was having an awful time of it. He wanted some whiskey so bad he thought he might go crazy with longing for it. He missed his house and his street and the dark, noisy bars that made him feel safe. He hated himself, hated the other patients, hated the doctors and, especially, hated the hospital ward where he slept. His bed was one of a row of beds filled with men just like him—drunks. He hated his thin, narrow bed, the whole row of thin, narrow beds, and inside his mind he screamed, "Out! Out! Get me *out!*"

At the end of that first week, Jack awoke at dawn. The other men around him lay snoring and sighing in their sleep, and only Jack lay awake. He looked out at the smoky blue morning light and decided he had to escape. He *would* escape. What could they do to him? Throw him in jail? So what. He felt like a prisoner, anyway.

Jack lay in his bed, watching the morning come, and thought about the things he had lost in his life. Too much, he thought. Too much.

Then, as he stared at the window in sadness, he saw something move, just at the edge of the sill.

He sat up quickly. Some kind of animal. A cat? He reached for his glasses and his pants.

Jack tiptoed over to the window and looked out to the far edge of the sill. Not a cat—it was a squirrel. A black squirrel. The animal sat on its haunches and looked right back at him.

Jack leaned against the radiator, barely breathing. Then, while he and the squirrel looked each other over, two more black squirrels jumped from a nearby tree onto the sill. All three animals sat up on their haunches and looked at Jack through the window.

"*Well,*" Jack whispered. "*Well.*"

The staring among them went on for several minutes, until Jack's legs got tired and he went back to bed. He fell asleep and when he woke, the three squirrels were gone.

He felt better, though, and decided to stick it out in the hospital another day. So he talked to the doctors, cried some, ate terrible meatloaf for dinner and in the evening went to bed early, expecting to get up the next morning and just walk out of the place.

He woke up at dawn again. As soon as his eyes opened, he couldn't help looking over at the window before he pulled on his pants and packed his few things.

All three squirrels again sat on the sill. One had a nut and was gnawing at it furiously, while the other two sniffed around the windowpane.

Jack put on his glasses and tiptoed over.

"Well," he said.

The squirrels raised up on their haunches when he stood at the window, intently watching him. At first Jack couldn't figure what to do. Then he decided to feed them.

He opened the drawer of his bedside table and pulled out a couple of packs of Saltines. When he slid open the window, the squirrels didn't run away, and when he held out the crackers, each squirrel grabbed one and sat back to enjoy a free breakfast.

Jack chuckled to himself.

That day, too, he changed his mind about leaving the hospital. He was a little friendlier to the doctors, and he played a game of cards with another man, a Korean War veteran (Jack's war was World War II). He also hid some corn-cobs from dinner inside his pillowcase.

Jack woke up the next morning and fed the squirrels. They hopped right up to him and reached for the cobs. Two of them ate the food, but the third jumped down into the yard and buried his.

You'll never find it again, Jack silently told the squirrel. *Boy, are you going to look foolish.* He grinned and went back to bed.

Day after day Jack fed those squirrels. One morning the smallest of the three had a bloody scrape on its back and Jack fed it an extra cracker, then worried about it all day.

Jack grew stronger with each new morning. After about two weeks, he gave up altogether his plans for escaping. He wanted to stay. His body didn't torture him for whiskey, he was growing to like the doctors, a few of the men had become important friends to him (he found he enjoyed talking with them far better than he had with his wife) and, most important, he had three squirrels to greet every morning.

By the fifth week, Jack had gained weight, made plans for a camping trip with another man and was finally not as afraid of his life as before. The doctors said he could leave.

Jack wanted to be home again, to move around in his own small kitchen and fix a few things in the garage. He wanted to leave. But he wondered about his squirrels.

He moved out of the hospital, back home, and for the next four days woke up at dawn and thought about the squirrels. Then on the fifth day, an idea struck him.

Jack was at the hospital the next morning, before sunrise. He walked through the grass around to the wing of the building where his ward had been. All the windows looked alike to him, especially in the half-light, but when he saw three black shapes moving around outside one of them, he knew he was in the right place.

"Hey!" Jack called softly, standing below the window. "Hey! I'm outside now!"

The squirrels stopped moving and sat, listening sharply. Then one of them jumped off the sill into a tree.

"Hey!" Jack called again. He opened the bag

he was carrying and pulled out a long rope of peanuts. He shook it at them.

"Look what's for breakfast," he said.

The peanuts that Jack had strung together like popcorn clicked in the silent yard, and the squirrels came after them.

Jack draped the rope over a few tree branches and watched, grinning, as the squirrels picked off the nuts.

"Thanks," he whispered. "Next week, sunflower seeds."

Stray

In January, a puppy wandered onto the property of Mr. Amos Lacey and his wife, Mamie, and their daughter, Doris. Icicles hung three feet or more from the eaves of houses, snowdrifts swallowed up automobiles and the birds were so fluffed up they looked comic.

The puppy had been abandoned, and it made its way down the road toward the Laceys' small house, its ears tucked, its tail between its legs, shivering.

Doris, whose school had been called off because of the snow, was out shoveling the cinderblock front steps when she spotted the pup on the road. She set down the shovel.

"Hey! Come on!" she called.

The puppy stopped in the road, wagging its tail timidly, trembling with shyness and cold.

Doris trudged through the yard, went up the shoveled drive and met the dog.

"Come on, Pooch."

"Where did *that* come from?" Mrs. Lacey asked as soon as Doris put the dog down in the kitchen.

Mr. Lacey was at the table, cleaning his fingernails with his pocketknife. The snow was keeping him home from his job at the warehouse.

"I don't know where it came from," he said mildly, "but I know for sure where it's going."

Doris hugged the puppy hard against her. She said nothing.

Because the roads would be too bad for travel for many days, Mr. Lacey couldn't get out to take the puppy to the pound in the city right away. He agreed to let it sleep in the basement while Mrs. Lacey grudgingly let Doris feed it table scraps. The woman was sensitive about throwing out food.

By the looks of it, Doris figured the puppy was about six months old, and on its way to being a big dog. She thought it might have some shepherd in it.

Four days passed and the puppy did not complain. It never cried in the night or howled at the wind. It didn't tear up everything in the basement. It wouldn't even follow Doris up the basement steps unless it was invited.

It was a good dog.

Several times Doris had opened the door in the kitchen that led to the basement and the puppy had been there, all stretched out, on the top step. Doris knew it had wanted some company and that it had lain against the door, listening to the talk in the kitchen, smelling the food, being a part of things. It always wagged its tail, eyes all sleepy, when she found it there.

Even after a week had gone by, Doris didn't name the dog. She knew her parents wouldn't let her keep it, that her father made so little money any pets were out of the question, and that the pup would definitely go to the pound when the weather cleared.

Still, she tried talking to them about the dog at dinner one night.

"She's a good dog, isn't she?" Doris said, hoping one of them would agree with her.

Her parents glanced at each other and went on eating.

"She's not much trouble," Doris added. "I like her." She smiled at them, but they continued to ignore her.

"I figure she's real smart," Doris said to her mother. "I could teach her things."

Mrs. Lacey just shook her head and stuffed a forkful of sweet potato in her mouth. Doris fell silent, praying the weather would never clear.

But on Saturday, nine days after the dog had arrived, the sun was shining and the roads were plowed. Mr. Lacey opened up the trunk of his car and came into the house.

Doris was sitting alone in the living room, hugging a pillow and rocking back and forth on the edge of a chair. She was trying not to cry but she was not strong enough. Her face was wet and red, her eyes full of distress.

Mrs. Lacey looked into the room from the doorway.

"Mama," Doris said in a small voice. "Please."

Mrs. Lacey shook her head.

"You know we can't afford a dog, Doris. You try to act more grown-up about this."

Doris pressed her face into the pillow.

Outside, she heard the trunk of the car slam shut, one of the doors open and close, the old engine cough and choke and finally start up.

"Daddy," she whispered. "Please."

She heard the car travel down the road, and, though it was early afternoon, she could do nothing but go to her bed. She cried herself to sleep, and her dreams were full of searching and searching for things lost.

It was nearly night when she finally woke up. Lying there, like stone, still exhausted, she wondered if she would ever in her life have anything. She stared at the wall for a while.

But she started feeling hungry, and she knew she'd have to make herself get out of bed and eat some dinner. She wanted not to go into the kitchen, past the basement door. She wanted not to face her parents.

But she rose up heavily.

Her parents were sitting at the table, dinner over, drinking coffee. They looked at her when she came in, but she kept her head down. No one spoke.

Doris made herself a glass of powdered milk

46

and drank it all down. Then she picked up a cold biscuit and started out of the room.

"You'd better feed that mutt before it dies of starvation," Mr. Lacey said.

Doris turned around.

"What?"

"I said, you'd better feed your dog. I figure it's looking for you."

Doris put her hand to her mouth.

"You didn't take her?" she asked.

"Oh, I took her all right," her father answered. "Worst looking place I've ever seen. Ten dogs to a cage. Smell was enough to knock you down. And they give an animal six days to live. Then they kill it with some kind of a shot."

Doris stared at her father.

"I wouldn't leave an *ant* in that place," he said. "So I brought the dog back."

Mrs. Lacey was smiling at him and shaking her head as if she would never, ever, understand him.

Mr. Lacey sipped his coffee.

"Well," he said, "are you going to feed it or not?"

Planting Things

Mr. Willis was a man who enjoyed planting things. He had several beds of zinnias, a large circle of green onions, a couple of barrels of eggplants, a row of spinach and some Swedish ivy on his front porch. Mr. Willis was not a practical gardener, so it did not matter to him whether or not he could eat what he grew, or even if what he planted grew badly or not at all. Mr. Willis just enjoyed planting things.

Mr. Willis's wife lived with him and she was not well. She was old (as was he, but it didn't seem to bother him so much), and she lay in bed most of every day. Mr. Willis loved her— he had loved her for fifty-six years—and he tended to her needs. Her favorite food was a chocolate milkshake mixed up with an egg and some powdered malt. He fixed one for her twice a day—and more, if she asked.

Mr. Willis missed his wife as he puttered about his yard, planting his favorite things. Sometimes she would pull herself up from her bed and stand at the window, watching him work among his onions or zinnias. But not often. She did not seem to enjoy life any longer since she had become old, as if she had decided there was no more for her to do. And Mr. Willis, as hard as he might try, could not change this.

On summer evenings, if the mosquitoes weren't too bad, Mr. Willis sat on his front porch and listened to the sound of children playing at the house just down the road. Traffic was light, and he could hear the crickets and the katydids in his apple trees. Sometimes he almost forgot, sitting there, that Mrs. Willis was in the house.

On his porch, Mr. Willis's Swedish ivy, growing down from a pot attached to the ceiling, was so healthy that Mr. Willis did not tend to it as he did his other growing things. Plucking off a brown leaf or two, that was all the plant required, and Mr. Willis could ignore it for days.

But on one summer evening, when there was still light enough outside to show up a brown leaf for plucking, Mr. Willis's Swedish ivy gave him the surprise of his life. He was glad he was on good terms with God, in case it should be a sign to him!

On top of the pot, among the ivy, a robin had built her nest. Right there, on the porch of Mr. Henry P. Willis, she had nested. There were plenty of trees about, but no, she had chosen to grow her babies on his porch.

Mr. Willis had thought at first she was one of those stuffed birds used to decorate Christmas trees or Easter bonnets. He thought someone had tricked him.

Still, being a cautious man, he had not reached for the bird but had moved closer, eye-level with her. And he knew then she was real. Real and sitting on eggs.

"Charlotte!" He went right to his wife's bedroom. "Charlotte!"

She was lying on her back, looking up at the ceiling. The room was gray.

"Charlotte, you will never believe this. There is a *bird* nesting in the Swedish ivy!" Mr. Willis's face was the brightest object in the room. She could see it shining. He took hold of her hand.

"It's a robin, dear," he said. "A *robin*. And she has eggs. I stood right beside her—can you believe it!"

Mrs. Willis smiled slightly.

"I'm happy for you, dear," she said.

Mr. Willis rubbed the top of her hand.

"Would you like to see?" he asked.

"I don't think so right now."

So Mr. Willis went back out to the porch, quietly closing the door behind him, and he sat down softly in his chair and watched the bird, feeling his heart pound in his chest.

The following morning Mr. Willis went to check the nest. The bird was away, and he saw three blue eggs lying in the nest, Swedish ivy bunched all around and spilling from the pot. Mr. Willis knew not to touch the eggs. He went on to his chores and waited for the robin to return.

After he had given his wife her morning milkshake, he asked her again, gently propping up the pillows behind her head, "Would you like to see the nest, dear?"

Mrs. Willis smiled and patted his hand. "I'll see it. Don't worry. I'll see it soon."

"Would you like to see it now? Can I help you out to the porch?"

Mrs. Willis sighed. "No, thank you, dear. I'll just lie here and rest a while. You go on. Don't worry about me."

Mr. Willis left her, worrying about her as he did nearly every minute he was awake. He pulled up some onions, watered the eggplant and checked the nest again.

The robin was back, sitting like a statue, never moving her head or blinking an eye, no matter how near Mr. Willis stood. Her being there on his porch among his ivy took his breath away.

One day Mrs. Willis stood at the front door and finally did see the bird, to satisfy her husband. She said she found the bird's being there "curious" and went back to bed.

Mr. Willis spent many summer evenings sitting on the porch with the robin. He never told anyone else about her, never pointed her out to visitors, for he feared that someone might frighten her or touch her eggs or steal her nest. He had learned that she would not leave her nest to protect herself.

Sitting with her, day after day, was like waiting for a baby to be born, as it had been for Mr. and Mrs. Willis when they were young and expecting their child. It had been quiet then, too, the waiting. The world had slowed down for them, and the days had been long and full of conversation. And finally their baby boy, Tom, had come.

Mr. Willis remembered this, sitting with the robin, and it gave him a feeling of great peace. He was sorry he and his wife had had only one child.

All three of the robin's eggs hatched sometime on a Thursday morning. Mr. Willis went to check on the nest after fixing his wife's breakfast, and he discovered the robin missing and three skinny, squawking babies.

"Well!" he said to them. "I'm a daddy!" He stood beside the nest, beaming.

In the days that followed, the mother robin was away from the nest most of the time, hunting for food. Mr. Willis wished he could make it easier for her—and he tried leaving popcorn and bread on the porch—but she was a particular mother and seemed to want only baby food he could not supply.

So he just sat with her babies, commending them on their fine growing bodies and scolding them for their constantly gaping mouths.

He sat in his chair and watched the birds and laughed out loud.

Mrs. Willis stood at the door once, watching her husband and his birds. She was surprised they had actually hatched, and she congratulated him.

"You have always done well with your planting, dear," she said. "Your Swedish ivy must have been good for them."

Then she went back to bed.

Mr. Willis had thought the birds would probably fly away from the nest one by one, as children do.

But one day, they were all gone, the mother and the children, and they did not come back.

It is probably best, thought Mr. Willis. Best they go all at once, with no long leave-takings and teary good-byes again and again.

But he did not miss them any the less, just because they had all flown in one morning. The empty nest stayed in the ivy until the winter, when he was sure they wouldn't be back.

He brought his chair and his ivy inside for the season, removing the nest and putting it on top of his dresser.

Mr. Willis would look after his wife all winter. Then, come spring, he would put the nest, ready-made, in one of his apple trees.

He was a man who enjoyed planting things.

A Bad Road for Cats

"Louie! Louis! Where are you?"

The woman called it out again and again as she walked along Route 6. A bad road for cats. She prayed he hadn't wandered this far. But it had been nearly two weeks, and still Louis hadn't come home.

She stopped at a Shell station, striding up to the young man at the register. Her eyes snapped black and fiery as she spit the question at him:

"Have you seen a *cat?*" The word *cat* came out hard as a rock.

The young man straightened up.

"No, ma'am. No cats around here. Somebody dropped a mutt off a couple nights ago, but a Mack truck got it yesterday about noon. Dog didn't have a chance."

The woman's eyes pinched his.

"I lost my cat. Orange and white. If you see him, you be more careful of him than that dog. This is a bad road for cats."

She marched toward the door.

"I'll be back," she said, like a threat, and the young man straightened up again as she went out.

"Louie! Louis! Where are you?"

She was a very tall woman, and skinny. Her black hair was long and shiny, like an Indian's. She might have been a Cherokee making her way alongside a river, alert and watchful. Tracking.

But Route 6 was no river. It was a truckers' road, lined with gas stations, motels, dairy bars, diners. A nasty road, smelling of diesel and rubber.

The woman's name was Magda. And she

was of French blood, not Indian. Magda was not old, but she carried herself as a very old and strong person might, with no fear of death and with a clear sense of her right to the earth and a disdain for the ugliness of belching machines and concrete.

Magda lived in a small house about two miles off Route 6. There she worked at a loom, weaving wool gathered from the sheep she owned. Magda's husband was dead, and she had no children. Only a cat named Louis.

Dunh. Dunh. Duuunnh.

Magda's heart pounded as a tank truck roared by. *Duuunnh.* The horn hurt her ears, making her feel sick inside, stealing some of her strength.

Four years before, Magda had found Louis at one of the gas stations on Route 6. She had been on her way home from her weekly trip to the grocery and had pulled in for a fill-up. As she'd stood inside the station in front of the cigarette machine, dropping in quarters, she'd felt warm fur against her leg and had given a start. Looking down, she'd seen an orange-and-white kitten. It had purred and meowed and pushed its nose into Magda's shoes. Smiling, Magda had picked the kitten up. Then she had seen the horror.

Half of the kitten's tail was gone. What remained was bloody and scabbed, and the stump stuck straight out.

Magda had carried the animal to one of the station attendants.

"Whose kitten is this?" Her eyes drilled in the question.

The attendant had shrugged his shoulders.

"Nobody's. Just a drop-off."

Magda had moved closer to him.

"What happened to its *tail*?" she asked, the words slow and clear.

"Got caught in the door. Stupid cat was under everybody's feet—no wonder half its tail got whacked."

Magda could not believe such a thing.

"And you offer it no *help*?" she had asked.

"Not my cat," he answered.

Magda's face had blazed as she'd turned and stalked out the door with the kitten.

A veterinarian mended what was left of the kitten's tail. And Magda named it Louis for her grandfather.

"Louie! Louis! Where are you?"

Dunh. Duuunnh. Another horn at her back. Magda wondered about her decision to walk Route 6 rather than drive it. She had thought that on foot she might find Louis more easily— in a ditch, under some bushes, up a tree. They were even, she and Louis, if she were on foot, too. But the trucks were making her misery worse.

Magda saw a dairy bar up ahead. She thought she would stop and rest. She would have some coffee and a slice of quiet away from the road.

She walked across the wide gravel lot to the tiny walk-up window. Pictures of strawberry sundaes, spongy shakes, cones with curly peaks were plastered all over the building, drawing business from the road with big red words like *CHILLY*.

Magda barely glanced at the young girl working inside. All teenage girls looked alike to her.

"Coffee," she ordered.

"Black?"

"Yes."

Magda moved to one side and leaned against the building. The trucks were rolling out on the highway, but far enough away to give her time to regain her strength. No horns, no smoke, no dirt. A little peace.

She drank her coffee and thought about Louis when he was a kitten. Once, he had leaped from her attic window and she had found him, stunned and shivering, on the hard gravel below. The veterinarian said Louis had broken a leg and was lucky to be alive. The kitten had stomped around in a cast for a few weeks. Magda drew funny faces on it to cheer him up.

Louis loved white cheese, tall grass and the skeins of wool Magda left lying around her loom.

That's what she would miss most, she thought, if Louis never came back: an orange and white cat making the yarn fly under her loom.

Magda finished her coffee, then turned to throw the empty cup in the trash can. As she did, a little sign in the bottom corner of the window caught her eye. The words were surrounded by dirty smudges:

4 Sal. CAT

Magda caught her breath. She moved up to the window and this time looked squarely into the face of the girl.

———

61

"Are you selling a *cat*?" she said quietly, but hard on *cat*.

"Not me. This boy," the girl answered, brushing her stringy hair back from her face.

"Where is he?" Magda asked.

"That yellow house right off the road up there."

Magda headed across the lot.

She had to knock only once. The door opened and standing there was a boy about fifteen.

"I saw your sign," Magda said. "I am interested in your cat."

The boy did not answer. He looked at Magda's face with his wide blue eyes, and he grinned, showing a mouth of rotten and missing teeth.

Magda felt a chill move over her.

"The cat," she repeated. "You have one to sell? Is it orange and white?"

The boy stopped grinning. Without a word, he slammed the door in Magda's face.

She was stunned. A strong woman like her, to be so stunned by a boy. It shamed her. But again she knocked on the door—and very hard this time.

No answer.

What kind of boy is this? Magda asked herself. A strange one. And she feared he had Louis.

She had just raised her hand to knock a third time when the door opened. There the boy stood with Louis in his arms.

Again, Magda was stunned. Her cat was covered with oil and dirt. He was thin, and his head hung weakly. When he saw Magda, he seemed to use his last bit of strength to let go a pleading cry.

The boy no longer was grinning. He held Louis close against him, forcefully stroking the cat's ears again and again and again. The boy's eyes were full of tears, his mouth twisted into sad protest.

Magda wanted to leap for Louis, steal him and run for home. But she knew better. This was an unusual boy. She must be careful.

Magda put her hand into her pocket and pulled out a dollar bill.

"Enough?" she asked, holding it up.

The boy clutched the cat harder, his mouth puckering fiercely.

Magda pulled out two more dollar bills. She held the money up, the question in her eyes.

The boy relaxed his hold on Louis. He tilted his head to one side, as if considering Magda's offer.

Then, in desperation, Magda pulled out a twenty-dollar bill.

"Enough?" she almost screamed.

The boy's head jerked upright, then he grabbed all the bills with one hand and shoved Louis at Magda with the other.

Magda cradled Louis in her arms, rubbing her cheek across his head. Before walking away, she looked once more at the boy. He stood stiffly with the money clenched in his hand, tears running from his eyes and dripping off his face like rainwater.

Magda took Louis home. She washed him and healed him. And for many days she was in a rage at the strange boy who had sold her her own cat, nearly dead.

When Louis was healthy, though, and his old fat self, playing games among the yarn beneath her loom, her rage grew smaller and smaller until finally she could forgive the strange boy.

She came to feel sympathy for him, remembering his tears. And she wove some orange and white wool into a pattern, stuffed it with cotton, sewed two green button eyes and a small pink mouth onto it, then attached a matching stub of a tail.

She put the gift in a paper bag, and, on her way to the grocery one day, she dropped the bag in front of the boy's yellow house.

Safe

When Denny visited his uncle in Maine, he came upon the cows one night and that changed him.

Denny lived in Canton, Ohio, with his mother, who was a playwright. She also worked every day at the newspaper company, but if asked what her work was, she would say play writing. Denny waited with her for the day one of her plays would sell to a big theater.

In the meantime, she kept her newspaper

job, Denny went to school and they lived in an apartment building.

The year Denny was in sixth grade, his uncle, a doctor, bought a farm in Maine, and Denny and his mother drove up there when school ended, to stay a few weeks. Denny watched the map as they drove north, and at times he felt they were driving straight to the edge of the world, risking a drop into Nothing. But when they finally crossed the Maine state line, strangely enough, he felt safer than he ever had before. The rest of the country might blow up, but in Maine he would be safe. He thought it might be all the spruce trees or the sky seeming so much closer to him, but he really did feel he was at the very edge of something and that it was safe.

Denny's Uncle Jim, who had never married, lived alone in a long, white frame house that attached itself to a barn. His job as a doctor prevented him from doing any real farming, but he kept a few chickens, a few pigs and a few cows. He hired a man to help care for the animals each morning and evening.

Uncle Jim was quiet, like Denny's mother, and, like her, he talked frankly with Denny about things they both might be interested in. In the evenings after dinner, the three of them would sit in Jim's living room and watch the news, then talk a while. Denny was not surprised when at the end of their first week, his mother and Uncle Jim started in about bombs and the end of the world.

Denny's mother had joined the Nuclear Freeze campaign a few months before they left for Maine. She had told Denny she was afraid for his future, that the earth might be destroyed if there were a nuclear war. "And what kind of war could there be but nuclear?" she would ask. "There's bound to be another big war," she'd add. "There have been two already."

Denny had listened seriously to all she had to say, but he hadn't talked about it with her.

In Canton, Ohio, nuclear war was possible. He knew it and he had already made a plan in case of an attack. He knew exactly where he would run if he were at school (to the old post office five blocks away—it used to be a fallout shelter) or at home (to his neighbor's house, which was made of stone and had a huge basement). He would cover his mouth with wet towels. He knew he could easily carry four hundred granola bars in a laundry bag. He worried about water to drink, though.

In Maine, Denny felt he had escaped, and for a few weeks could forget about the bomb. But with their evening talks, his mother and his uncle were not giving him a chance.

When he first arrived at the farm, Denny had visited the barn, interested to see the chickens, pigs and cows. But as soon as he discovered the lake up the road and was given a fishing pole by Uncle Jim, he forget the farm and spent most of every day on the water. His mother stayed in the cool, dark kitchen and worked on a play.

While he fished, Denny tried to forget things. But sometimes he would suddenly imagine himself running in the path of a fireball, or his mother screaming as the newspaper building shattered all around her. He wondered if anyone would hear the bomb as it fell.

Denny wanted to talk to someone about these things, but there was no one he could trust. He knew his mother would make him feel more afraid. His Uncle Jim might think him a coward. And anyone else might lie and tell him he had nothing to worry about.

One evening after dinner and the news, when his mother and Uncle Jim started in on a doctor's responsibility and the Nuclear Freeze, Denny decided that being by himself would be better. He left them and went walking across the farmyard.

That night, the cows were there. It was nearly dark outside, but just enough light was left to walk without a flashlight and to see the shapes of things. Denny saw the five cows standing up against the fence surrounding the barn, and he went to them.

It was quiet, growing dark, and the farm was so thick with life. . . . Denny walked very softly toward the cows. He was a little afraid of them and did not stand right up next to the fence.

They stood and they watched, those five cows—big heads and strong breath and curiosity.

Denny stood with them and felt very serious. He regarded them solemnly.

The cows' eyes were all large and shining and very, very peaceful. Denny stared at the eyes and he felt reassured. He felt stronger. He felt safe.

Denny moved up against the fence, and the cows wobbled among themselves a minute, then were still again. He put his hand through the fence and gently touched the muzzle of the cow nearest him. It watched him with soft eyes and did not move away.

Denny breathed deep and smiled and stood resting with the cows a long time. Then he went inside.

Afterward, every night when the talk in the house turned to nuclear war, Denny went to the cows. And they always made him feel safe.

It wasn't too many nights, though, until his mother and Uncle Jim noticed his leaving them alone. And when. They knew, finally, what subject could chase Denny out of the room.

One night, then, they came after him and found him with the cows.

"We have made you sad," they said. "Or maybe afraid. And we are sorry."

Denny didn't want to talk of it near the cows, so the three of them went back inside the house.

Denny didn't have to run to the cows any more nights after that. Sometimes, though, he went to see them while the news was on, or just before bed. He liked them so.

When the vacation ended and Denny returned to Canton with his mother, he noticed she was careful not to discuss the Nuclear

Freeze around him. It helped some, but not completely. He had learned enough to still be afraid.

And when he did feel afraid, he shut his eyes tight and walked across the yard in Maine to the cows.

Shells

"You *hate* living here."

Michael looked at the woman speaking to him.

"No, Aunt Esther. I don't." He said it dully, sliding his milk glass back and forth on the table. "I don't hate it here."

Esther removed the last pan from the dishwasher and hung it above the oven.

"You hate it here," she said, "and you hate me."

"I don't!" Michael yelled. "It's not you!"

The woman turned to face him in the kitchen.

"Don't yell at me!" she yelled. "I'll not have it in my home. I can't make you happy, Michael. You just refuse to be happy here. And you punish me every day for it."

"*Punish* you?" Michael gawked at her. "I don't punish you! I don't care about you! I don't care what you eat or how you dress or where you go or what you think. Can't you just leave me alone?"

He slammed down the glass, scraped his chair back from the table and ran out the door.

"Michael!" yelled Esther.

They had been living together, the two of them, for six months. Michael's parents had died and only Esther could take him in—or, only she had offered to. Michael's other relatives could not imagine dealing with a fourteen-year-old boy. They wanted peaceful lives.

Esther lived in a condominium in a wealthy section of Detroit. Most of the area's residents were older (like her) and afraid of the world they lived in (like her). They stayed indoors much of the time. They trusted few people.

Esther liked living alone. She had never

74

married or had children. She had never lived anywhere but Detroit. She liked her condominium.

But she was fiercely loyal to her family, and when her only sister had died, Esther insisted she be allowed to care for Michael. And Michael, afraid of going anywhere else, had accepted.

Oh, he was lonely. Even six months after their deaths, he still expected to see his parents—sitting on the couch as he walked into Esther's living room, waiting for the bathroom as he came out of the shower, coming in the door late at night. He still smelled his father's Old Spice somewhere, his mother's talc.

Sometimes he was so sure one of them was *somewhere* around him that he thought maybe he was going crazy. His heart hurt him. He wondered if he would ever get better.

And though he denied it, he did hate Esther. She was so different from his mother and father. Prejudiced—she admired only those who were white and Presbyterian. Selfish—she wouldn't allow him to use her phone. Complaining—she always had a headache or a backache or a stomachache.

He didn't want to, but he hated her. And he didn't know what to do except lie about it.

Michael hadn't made any friends at his new school, and his teachers barely noticed him. He came home alone every day and usually found Esther on the phone. She kept in close touch with several other women in nearby condominiums.

Esther told her friends she didn't understand Michael. She said she knew he must grieve for his parents, but why punish her? She said she thought she might send him away if he couldn't be nicer. She said she didn't deserve this.

But when Michael came in the door, she always quickly changed the subject.

One day after school Michael came home with a hermit crab. He had gone into a pet store, looking for some small living thing, and hermit crabs were selling for just a few dollars. He'd bought one, and a bowl.

Esther, for a change, was not on the phone when he arrived home. She was having tea and a crescent roll and seemed cheerful. Michael wanted badly to show someone what he had bought. So he showed her.

Esther surprised him. She picked up the shell

and poked the long, shiny nail of her little finger at the crab's claws.

"Where is he?" she asked.

Michael showed her the crab's eyes peering through the small opening of the shell.

"Well, for heaven's sake, come out of there!" she said to the crab, and she turned the shell upside down and shook it.

"Aunt Esther!" Michael grabbed for the shell.

"All right, all right." She turned it right side up. "Well," she said, "what does he do?"

Michael grinned and shrugged his shoulders.

"I don't know," he answered. "Just grows, I guess."

His aunt looked at him.

"An attraction to a crab is something I cannot identify with. However, it's fine with me if you keep him, as long as I can be assured he won't grow out of that bowl." She gave him a hard stare.

"He won't," Michael answered. "I promise."

The hermit crab moved into the condominium. Michael named him Sluggo and kept the bowl beside his bed. Michael had to watch the bowl for very long periods of time to catch Sluggo with his head poking out of his shell, moving around. Bedtime seemed to be Sluggo's liveliest part of the day, and Michael found it easy to lie and watch the busy crab as sleep slowly came on.

One day Michael arrived home to find Esther sitting on the edge of his bed, looking at the bowl. Esther usually did not intrude in Michael's room, and seeing her there disturbed him. But he stood at the doorway and said nothing.

Esther seemed perfectly comfortable, although she looked over at him with a frown on her face.

"I think he needs a companion," she said.

"What?" Michael's eyebrows went up as his jaw dropped down.

Esther sniffed.

"I think Sluggo needs a girl friend." She stood up. "Where is that pet store?"

Michael took her. In the store was a huge tank full of hermit crabs.

"Oh my!" Esther grabbed the rim of the tank and craned her neck over the side. "Look at them!"

Michael was looking more at his Aunt Esther than at the crabs. He couldn't believe it.

"Oh, look at those shells. You say they grow out of them? We must stock up with several sizes. See the pink in that one? Michael, look! He's got his little head out!''

Esther was so dramatic—leaning into the tank, her bangle bracelets clanking, earrings swinging, red pumps clicking on the linoleum—that she attracted the attention of everyone in the store. Michael pretended not to know her well.

He and Esther returned to the condominium with a thirty-gallon tank and twenty hermit crabs.

Michael figured he'd have a heart attack before he got the heavy tank into their living room. He figured he'd die and Aunt Esther would inherit twenty-one crabs and funeral expenses.

But he made it. Esther carried the box of crabs.

''Won't Sluggo be surprised?'' she asked happily. ''Oh, I do hope we'll be able to tell him apart from the rest. He's their founding father!''

Michael, in a stupor over his Aunt Esther and the phenomenon of twenty-one hermit crabs, wiped out the tank, arranged it with gravel and sticks (as well as the plastic scuba diver Aunt Esther insisted on buying) and assisted her in loading it up, one by one, with the new residents. The crabs were as over-whelmed as Michael. Not one showed its face.

Before moving Sluggo from his bowl, Aunt Esther marked his shell with some red finger-nail polish so she could distinguish him from the rest. Then she flopped down on the couch beside Michael.

"Oh, what would your mother *think*, Mi-chael, if she could see this mess we've gotten ourselves into!"

She looked at Michael with a broad smile, but it quickly disappeared. The boy's eyes were full of pain.

"Oh, my," she whispered. "I'm sorry."

Michael turned his head away.

Aunt Esther, who had not embraced anyone in years, gently put her arm about his shoul-ders.

"I am so sorry, Michael. Oh, you must hate me."

Michael sensed a familiar smell then. His mother's talc.

He looked at his aunt.

"No, Aunt Esther." He shook his head sol-emnly. "I don't hate you."

Esther's mouth trembled and her bangles

clanked as she patted his arm. She took a deep, strong breath.

"Well, let's look in on our friend Sluggo," she said.

They leaned their heads over the tank and found him. The crab, finished with the old home that no longer fit, was coming out of his shell.

Exciting fiction from three-time Newbery Honor author Gary Paulsen

Aladdin Paperbacks
Simon & Schuster Children's Publishing
www.SimonSaysKids.com

The Newbery Medal is awarded each year to the most distinguished
contribution to literature for children published in the U.S.
How many of these Newbery winners, available from
Aladdin Paperbacks, have you read?

Newbery Medal Winners

❑ *Caddie Woodlawn*
by Carol Ryrie Brink
0-689-81521-2

❑ *Hitty: Her First
Hundred Years*
by Rachel Field
0-689-82284-7

❑ *The Grey King*
by Susan Cooper
0-689-71089-5

❑ *Mrs. Frisby and the
Rats of NIMH* by
Robert C. O'Brien
0-689-71068-2

❑ *Call It Courage*
by Armstrong Sperry
0-02-045270-5

❑ *From the Mixed-up
Files of Mrs. Basil E.
Frankweiler*
by E. L. Konigsburg
0-689-71181-6

❑ *King of the Wind*
by Marguerite Henry
0-689-71486-6

❑ *Shadow of a Bull* by
Maia Wojciechowska
0-689-71567-6

❑ *The Cat Who Went
to Heaven* by
Elizabeth Coatsworth
0-698-71433-5

❑ *A Gathering of Days*
by Joan W. Blos
0-689-71419-X

❑ *M.C. Higgins,
the Great*
by Virginia Hamilton
0-02-043490-1

❑ *Smoky the Cow Horse*
by Eric P. Kelly
0-689-71682-6
$5.50 US / $8.99
Canadian

❑ *The View from Saturday*
by E. L. Konigsburg
0-689-81721-5

Newbery Honor Books

❑ *The Bears on
Hemlock Mountain*
by Alice Dalgliesh
0-689-71604-4

❑ *The Jazz Man*
by Mary Hays Weik
0-689-71767-9
$3.95 US / $4.95
Canadian

❑ *The Planet of Junior
Brown*
by Virginia Hamilton
0-689-71721-0

❑ *Misty of Chincoteague*
by Marguerite Henry
0-689-71492-0
The Moorchild
by Eloise McGraw
0-689-82033-X

❑ *Calico Bush*
by Rachel Field
0-689-82285-5

❑ *The Dark Is Rising*
by Susan Cooper
0-689-71087-9

❑ *Dogsong*
by Gary Paulsen
0-689-80409-1

❑ *The Courage of
Sarah Noble*
by Alice Dalgliesh
0-689-71540-4

❑ *A String in the Harp*
by Nancy Bond
0-689-80445-8
$5.99 US / $8.50
Canadian

❑ *Hatchet*
by Gary Paulsen
0-689-80882-8

❑ *Sugaring Time*
by Kathryn Lasky
0-689-71081-X
$5.99 US / $8.50
Canadian

❑ *Volcano*
by Patricia Lauber
0-689-71679-6
$8.99 US / $12.50
Canadian

❑ *The Golden Fleece*
by Padraic Colum
0-02-042260-1
$9.95 US / $13.50
Canadian

❑ *Justin Morgan
Had a Horse*
by Marguerite Henry
0-689-71534-X

❑ *Yolonda's Genius* by
Carol Fenner
0-689-81327-9
$5.50 US / $8.99
Canadian

All titles $4.99 US / $6.99 Canadian unless otherwise noted

Aladdin Paperbacks
Simon & Schuster Children's Publishing
www.SimonSaysKids.com